The Penguin and the Wallaby

By Andrew & Kimberley Barber

The Penguin and the Wallaby

By Andrew & Kimberley Barber

Illustrations by MassiveBrain
Special thanks to Carey Perez

Copyright © 2016 by Andrew Barber
ISBN-10: 1544659768
ISBN-13: 978-1544659763
First Edition Published 2017

Dale's Tale

My name is Dale.

My family lives in Halifax, Nova Scotia.
That's way up north in Canada.

Mom had to take a business trip to Melbourne, Australia.

That is on the far side of the world.
We made it into a family trip.

We flew for almost a whole day to get there.

We watched a movie, I read two books and I slept in my seat.

Australia's sun can be very fierce. We all bought hats so we wouldn't get sunburned.

Mine was blue and had an Australian flag on it.

After Mom finished her meetings
we took a tour to Phillip Island.

On the way, the bus stopped where there were lots of colorful
birds. We fed them and one landed on my blue hat.

We went to an animal preserve.

We saw a koala…

and an emu…

and an echidna…   and kangaroos.

I touched the kangaroo's nose
so now I think we are friends.

Then we saw a wallaby which is a small
sort of kangaroo or "Roo."

Then, just before sunset, we went to watch the penguins come ashore.

The Ranger told us how every night at sunset little blue penguins come ashore and cross the beach.

We had to sit still and be quiet because the penguins are easily frightened.

It was getting dark when we saw a penguin come ashore.

It started across the beach, but it got
scared and ran back into the water.

Then three penguins started to cross the beach. But the last penguin got scared and ran back to the water.

The first two looked behind them
and then they ran back too.

One penguin got all the way to the dunes. Then it turned around and ran all the way back to the water.

Dad laughed and said that was a
pretty silly thing for it to do.

It took a long time, but finally one
brave penguin crossed the beach.

I wanted to cheer, but I didn't want to scare it.

Soon lots of penguins were leaving the
water and crossing the beach.

The Ranger said some nights
two thousand penguins come ashore!

A lot of penguins fell down, but they just got up again. I guess they are used to it.

After the penguins had crossed the beach, we started back to the buses and we saw the penguin burrows.

Those are little holes and caves
they make in the ground to live in.

The penguins stood outside their burrows
and watched us leave.

As we walked by one burrow I saw
a penguin that seemed upset.

I guess it wanted to go into its burrow but there was
a wallaby eating grass and blocking its way.

I felt sorry for the poor penguin because it didn't seem to know what to do.

First it was just flapping its flippers. Then it walked in circles. Then it let out a loud squawk.

The wallaby kept eating grass. I don't think it even noticed the penguin was there. Finally, it hopped away.

I bet that penguin was glad to get back into its house!

It was a great day and because I had been quiet Mom and Dad bought me a stuffed penguin.

It was fun to watch all the penguins. I asked Mom and Dad if we could come back again the next day.

"Not this trip," they said, "because there are lots of other special things to see. Maybe on another trip."

That night I was very tired and fell asleep quickly.

I dreamed about the funny squawking
penguin and the wallaby.

Splasher's Tale

My name is Splasher.
I am a Little Blue Penguin

I live near the top of my world, but not with my cousins on the great ice. I live across the blue water where it is warmer.

Diver, my mate, and I take turns feeding in the blue water and bringing food back for our chicks.

I said goodbye to Diver and went off to hunt.

I swam for many days and nights catching fish to eat.

The blue water can be very dangerous, so our feathers are blue to help hide us from hungry sharks and seals.

Sometimes we watch the sky birds fly back to land.
We have flippers instead of wings.

They can fly but we are very strong swimmers.

Once I almost swam into another penguin.

We startled each other at first, but then we
laughed about it and became friends.

I had finished my hunting and felt nice and full.

I swam toward our home to feed our chicks and
let Diver go swim in the blue water and hunt.

I gathered with many other penguins off the shore.

I found my good friends Squawker and Moon Watcher.

We waited until the sun went down because it is safer to cross the wide sand in the dark. Every night many humans sit on the hill and look at the water.

I guess they want to go swimming, but are afraid to cross the wide sand. They are not as brave as we penguins are!

Squawker was the first to walk ashore.

He started across the wide sand, but he got nervous and ran back into the blue water.

I started across the wide sand with Moon Watcher and Squawker. But Squawker got nervous again and ran back into the blue water.

Moon Watcher followed Squawker and I followed Moon Watcher. Better safe than sorry.

Then Squawker ran out of the waves and almost reached the tall hill at the end of the wide sand.

But then he got nervous and ran all the way back to the edge of the blue water.

Moon Watcher was the first to cross the wide sand. I think she was too distracted watching the moon to get nervous.

And I know she really wanted to see her mate and chicks.

After Moon Watcher crossed the wide sand we all came out of the blue water in groups to stay safe.

A lot of us fell down once or twice.

We penguins are very mighty swimmers,
but when we walk we can be a little clumsy.

After I crossed the wide sand I went up the
tall hill and down the tall hill to my home.

And then I saw Diver and our chicks!
I had really missed them.

Instead of crossing the wide sand, the humans
always walk away from the blue water
to their big bright burrow.

We watch them every night.

Squawker got to his burrow, but there
was a wallaby blocking his entrance.

Squawker jumped up and down and yelled
"Go away! Go away, you stupid wallaby!
I need to feed my chicks."

At first the wallaby was too surprised to move.

Then it turned around and hopped away.
Squawker looked very pleased with himself.

Then Squawker ran into his burrow before
the wallaby could come back.

When the wallaby left I saw it had been standing on a pebble. I took it into the burrow and gave it to Diver and our chicks because it was pretty.

And it would remind me of
Squawker and the wallaby.

Our family watched the people leave. One of the chicks asked if we could watch the humans the next night.

"Of course!" I said. "People do this every night.
Not even the wisest penguin knows why."

I fed our chicks and they quickly fell asleep. I stepped outside to check that all was quiet. The humans were gone and the wallaby had not come back. Moon Watcher was watching the moon set.

From the next burrow I could hear Squawker telling his story to his chicks: "You go away you big wallaby!"

About the....

Kimberley and Andrew Barber
live near Washington DC.

They visited Phillip Island and there really was
a wallaby blocking a penguin's front door.

Authors.

Splasher lives on Phillip Island
with Diver and their two chicks.

The whole family likes to watch the humans every night.
This is Splasher's first book.

Made in the USA
Middletown, DE
29 April 2017